The Best Fish Ever

The Drama Club
is having tryouts for

The Fisherman and His Four Wishes

November 17   3:30 PM

by Julio Varela

illustrated by Eric Velasquez

HOUGHTON MIFFLIN   BOSTON

Too Excited to Eat

It was only 7:30 A.M., but Manny was almost out the door. Ever since he started fourth grade three months ago, he had been waiting for this day to come.

"Mom, don't forget," Manny called on his way out. "Today after school I'll be with the Drama Club. We're having tryouts for the play."

"I know, I know," Manny's mom said. "You've been talking about it for the last three months. You're not having breakfast?"

"I'm too excited to eat," said Manny. "See you later!"

"Good luck!" Manny's mom said as she closed the door.

As he waited for the elevator, all Manny could think about was the tryouts.

This year Mr. Greene, the drama teacher, turned the story "The Fisherman and His Four Wishes" into a play. The play had only three main characters — the fisherman, his wife, and the magic fish who could grant wishes.

Mr. Greene wrote a happy ending for the play. When the fisherman loses everything because of his foolish wishes, the fish feels sorry for him and grants him a *fourth* wish. Luckily, the fisherman has finally learned his lesson and wishes for something of real value.

It was going to be a great play. More than anything, Manny wanted to play the part of the fisherman.

Who will Be the Fisherman?

"Mr. Greene says I would make a good fisherman," Manny said to his best friend, Nick.

Nick looked up from his tuna sandwich. He took a sip of milk before talking to his friend. "Are you forgetting something? You still have to try out. I mean, everyone wants to be the fisherman. Marcus, Guillermo, Richie, Ahmad, even Elena," Nick said.

"I know, but come on, you know I'm the best," Manny said. "I already know all the lines."

"I still think you should wait until you try out. What if you don't get it?" Nick asked.

"Yeah, right," Manny said, as if there were no chance of disappointment.

Nick shrugged his shoulders and went back to his sandwich.

The Drama Club
is having tryouts for

The Fisherman and His Four Wishes

November 17   3:30 PM

The Tryouts

After school, Manny sat with the other Drama Club members and listened to Mr. Greene's instructions. "Okay, everyone, thanks for coming. When I call your name, please join me in the other room. You'll read your lines to me in there."

"Too bad," Manny thought. "Everyone but Mr. Greene will miss my tryout performance."

First Mr. Greene called Elena, then
Marcus, Richie, Guillermo, and Ahmad. Finally
he called, "Manny Rodríguez."

Manny bolted from his seat, looked around
to see how many others were waiting, and
shouted, "Yes, sir, I'm ready!"

Mr. Greene gave Manny a script. Then he said, "Okay, Manny, in this scene you will read the part of the fisherman, and I will read the part of the fish. This is when the fisherman makes the wish to live in a castle. Ready? Let's go."

Manny began to read his lines. He knew every one of them by heart. This was too easy.

The Telephone Call

That night Manny sat at the kitchen table, trying to do his math homework. But all he could think about was Mr. Greene announcing, "Manny Rodríguez will be the fisherman."

Suddenly, the phone rang, jolting Manny from his daydream. It was Mr. Greene. "Manny, you did a good job today, and I've decided to give you the part of . . ."

This is it, Manny thought. Say it's the fisherman.

". . . the fish."

"The *what?*" Manny yelped. "But Mr. Greene, I *really* want to be the fisherman. I know all the lines."

"So do a lot of the other kids," said Mr. Greene. "I gave that part to Ahmad. I think he'll make a great fisherman. *You* are going to make a great fish. Besides, the fish has the funniest lines in the play."

Mr. Greene took a deep breath and went on. "Manny, you are lucky. Lots of kids won't even be in the play. If you'd rather not play the fish, I'm sure I can find someone who will."

Manny didn't know what to say, and for a moment he was quiet. Then he said goodbye to Mr. Greene.

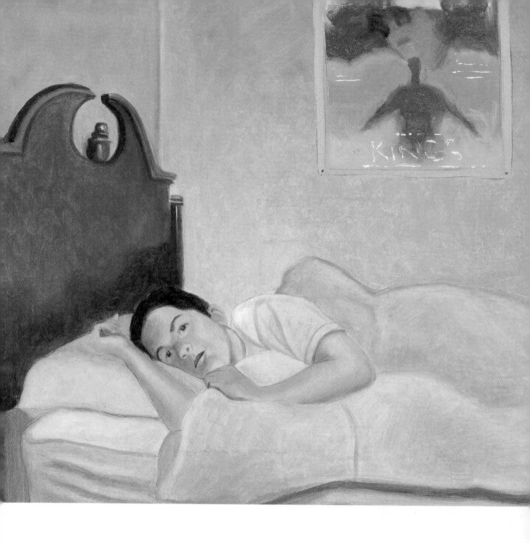

As he got ready for bed, Manny told his mom what had happened. "It's just not fair," Manny said.

"Manny," said his mom, "just think about what Mr. Greene said. You want to be in the play. You're lucky to have been chosen."

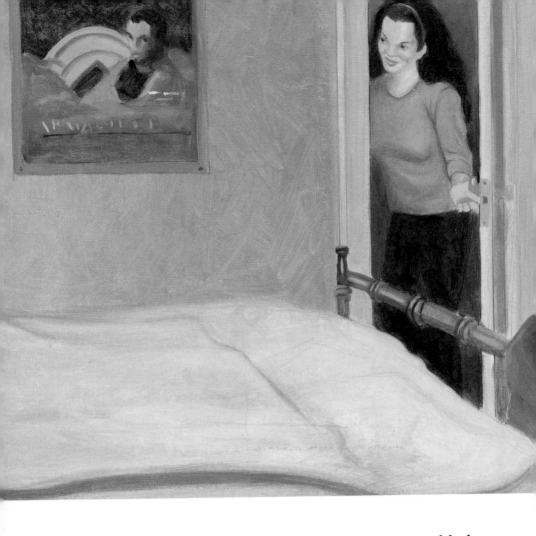

"Yeah, I'll think about it," Manny grumbled.
"Good night."

The Play

Six weeks had passed, and the first performance of "The Fisherman and His Four Wishes" had finally arrived. It seemed as if the whole school was there. As the curtain rose and the play began, Mr. Greene looked proudly at his actors. He was right — Ahmad was a great fisherman. Everyone in the audience thought so the moment he walked on the stage.

But on that afternoon, the audience's favorite was the fish. Manny flopped around the stage and said his funny fish lines. He did just what he told himself over the past six weeks. "If I have to be a fish, then I'll be the best fish ever!"

When the play ended, Manny heard
nothing but cheers.

Mr. Greene told everyone that the play was
a success because of their efforts. "I hope you'll
all try out for the play next year."

"I know I will," Manny said. "But can I
play a person next time?"